POCKET
HEROES

SIR LANCE
A-LITTLE

For my son, Gregory – a real life pocket hero
D.W.

For Ross, Ray and Charlie – three brave men, indeed
C.I.

ORCHARD BOOKS
338 Euston Road, London NW1 3BH
Orchard Books Australia
Level 17/207 Kent Street, Sydney, NSW 2000

First published in 2013
First paperback publication in 2014

ISBN 978 1 40831 354 1 (hardback)
ISBN 978 1 40831 360 2 (paperback)

A CIP catalogue record for this book is available
from the British Library.

1 3 5 7 9 10 8 6 4 2 (hardback)
1 3 5 7 9 10 8 6 4 2 (paperback)

Printed in Great Britain

Orchard Books is a division of Hachette Children's Books,
an Hachette UK company.

www.hachette.co.uk

SIR LANCE A-LITTLE

DAVE WOODS
CHRIS INNS

ORCHARD

Knights, as we know, have always been famous for their courage. But before knights were knights – they were squires. And there was one young squire who was as brave as brave could be (perhaps even braver).

His name was *Sir Lance-a-Little*!

A long time ago, knights roamed the land.

And when knights weren't roaming the land, they were busy telling tales about their adventures. Their favourite place to meet was on a bridge in London.

It was called *Knightsbridge*.

One fine day – legend says – a new knight came to Knightsbridge. He was a young knight, hungry for adventure, with a lance in one hand and a packed lunch in the other.

He went by the name of Sir Lance-a-Little.

"GOOD MORNING, GOOD KNIGHTS!" cried Sir Lance-a-Little. There was a rattle of armour as great knights looked up from telling even greater stories.

"Er, pardon?" said a large, barrel-chested knight. It was Sir Flagon of Ale.

"My name is Sir Lance-a-Little." Sir Lance-a-Little pulled out a list (which was longer than he was).

"I AM ON A QUEST!" cried the little knight.

"Short trip, is it?" grinned Sir Flagon.

There was a ripple of laughter.

"I HAVE NO TIME TO WASTE!" exclaimed Sir Lance-a-Little.

"Yes," agreed Sir Reginald Rustybottom. "Time is short!"

More tinny tittering.

"To complete my quest," Sir Lance-a-Little continued, in a small but noble voice, "I need some brave knights to join me!"

A hush fell over the knights. Laughter ceased. For the one thing knights take seriously (more seriously even than new anti-rust products) is a chance to prove their bravery.

But before anyone could step forward, Sir Lance-a-Little's eye was drawn to one group of knights in particular…

A group that huddled together fiercely.

"Ah, brave knights!" said Sir Lance-a-Little. "I see you are united by courage!"

(Actually, it was fear.)

"And your swords shake in readiness for the quest!" he added.

(No, they were just scared.)

"What do they call thee?" asked Sir Lance-a-Little.

"They call us... *THE COWARDS OF CAMELOT!*" said Quaver the Minstrel, their travelling musician.

"Then ride with me, Cowards of Camelot!" Sir Lance-a-Little checked his Quest List. "We shall fight terrible ogres..."

The Cowards took a step backwards.

"We shall defeat evil wizards..." the little knight continued.

The Cowards took another step back.

"We shall slay fierce dragons..."
And another step back.

"We shall, er…"

Sir Lance-a-Little thought for
a moment – then continued.

"We shall…eat cake!"

"CAKE?" said Sir Render, one of the
Cowards, as they all stepped forward.
"What sort of cake?"

"Oh, chocolate muffins. Fondant
fancies. Typical banquet-type treats
you get at the end of a quest," said
Sir Lance-a-Little.

"And puddings, too?" asked Sir Hugo
First.

"Verily," said Sir Lance-a-Little.
"With custard!"

(Verily is a knight's way of saying 'yes'.)

The Cowards had a hurried huddle.
Then they came forward again.

WIDE LOAD

"We're in!" they whispered.

And they were. Because they may have been cowardly – but they loved their custard!

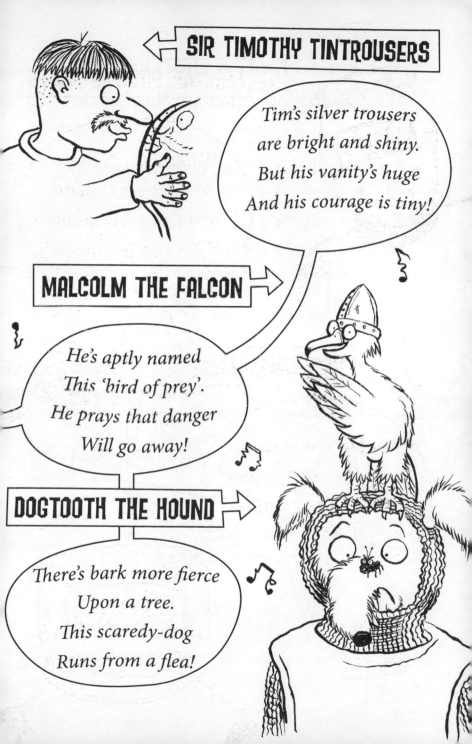

So began Sir Lance-a-Little's quest, with
the Cowards of Camelot riding beside
him.

(Well, behind him, actually.)

Sir Lance-a-Little checked his
Quest List.

"The first task is tricky," he said.
"We need to defeat a wizard."

"An evil wizard?" squawked
Sir Percival Poop-de-Pants.

"Verily," replied the little knight.
"The sort of wizard that puts the evil
in medieval."

"Oh, dear…" said Sir Render.

Sir Lance-a-Little pulled a copy of 'Which Wizard?' from his saddlebag. "We must head to the village of Magic Wandsworth. Apparently, there's an evil wizard there."

So they did.

And there was.

He was called GONDAFT THE WIZARD.

(He'd gone daft by mixing up his spellbooks with his cookbooks. And as he was a very bad cook – his magic was very bad, too.)

"GONDAFT THE WIZARD!" yelled Sir Lance-a-Little. "You have cooked up nothing but trouble – and a few dozen wing-of-bat-flavoured pastries – for the people of Camelot. Get thee gone!"

"I AM NOT GOING ANYWHERE! I SHALL COOK A SPELL UPON THEE!" raged Gondaft. (Evil wizards say that sort of thing.)

He pointed his wooden spoon at the cowardly knights. The air began to crackle with magic (and the smell of fried onions).

"ABRA-KEBABRA!
KNIGHT, FALCON, DOG.
I'LL CHANGE YOU TO CAKES
EACH SHAPED LIKE A FROG!"

Gondaft's spoon sizzled and a bolt
of delicious-smelling magic drifted
towards Sir Lance-a-Little.

But, at the last moment, the little
knight pulled Sir Timothy Tintrousers
in front of him. The vain knight's super-
shiny armour reflected the evil wizard's
cookery spell straight back at him!

Hey Pesto! Gondaft was turned
into a cream-filled, frog-shaped cake.

"Well, he got his just desserts," said Sir Timothy Tintrousers.

Sir Lance-a-Little agreed, then put a cherry on top of Gondaft – and a big tick on his Quest List!

Sir Timothy's trousers
Were shiny and bright.
Now Gondaft's a frog
And Sir Lance still a knight!

"Next," read Sir Lance-
a-Little, "we must save a
DAMSEL IN DISTRESS!"

So they searched high and
low for a tower (well, mainly
high) until they found one.

It was very white and
very tall.

(But mainly, very tall.)

"SAVE ME!" cried a
Damsel in Distress from
the upper window.

SAVE ME!

(Damsels in Distress always
say that.)

"Er, we're scared of heights!" pointed out the Cowards. (No surprise there.)

Sir Cumference held his long lance up to the tower to show just how high it was…

And suddenly, Sir Lance-a-Little was scurrying up the lance like a little metal-plated monkey!

Up he climbed.

Higher.

Higher.

Dangerously higher.

Until – he reached the tower
window!

The Cowards burst into
applause. (Which made a change from
them bursting into tears.)

"I'm Alice from the Palace!" squealed the delighted Damsel. Then she gave Sir Lance-a-Little a big, slobbery kiss.

Yuk! he thought. (Knights don't do kissing.)

"Come, my lady," he said. "We must away!"

"Are we going somewhere?" she asked. "I must change – I can't go out in my dressing-gown!"

"We're in a hurry, my lady," urged Sir Lance-a-Little, trying to be polite. "You see, I'm on a quest..."

"Not so fast, junior!" snapped Alice. "I've got an important decision to make."

"An important decision?"

She grabbed two outfits from her wardrobe. "Now, should I be a Damsel in Dis-dress? Or Dat-dress?"

Sir Lance-a-Little nodded politely... and backed towards the window.

Alice pulled out more dresses. "Now, let me think..."

Sir Lance-a-Little slid back down
Sir Cumference's lance.

"There are
soooooooo many
choices," continued Alice.
And she was still chattering to herself
as the cowardly knights – led by Sir
Lance-a-Little – rode away.

"She seemed nice, didn't she?" said Sir Render. "But in the end she was a bit of an Ogre…"

"Funny you should mention OGRES," grinned Sir Lance-a-Little, checking his list, "because that's our next challenge!"

"Oh, dear…" said Sir Render.

The Damsel so fair
Was trapped in the tower.
But Lance got distressed
By her kick-butt girl power!

Later, the band of knights approached
a large stone bridge.

From underneath it came a terrible roar.

"ROOOOOOAAAAAAARRRR!"

(Told you it was terrible.)

The terrible roar was accompanied
by a terrible Ogre. (Which made sense.)

"For you to pass over my bridge,"
growled the Ogre, "I must eat the bravest
amongst you!"

(Ogres are partial to brave knights. Peeled, of course.)

Sir Lance-a-Little whispered something to Sir Hugo First. The cowardly knight then edged nervously onto the bridge…

"Oh, don't eat me, Mr Ogre," cried Sir Hugo. "There's a much braver, and therefore more delicious knight behind me…"

"Very well, pass then!" bellowed the ogre.

Next up was Lady Gwyneth Fear. "Don't eat me either, Mr Ogre. For following me is a knight so brave, he's truly scrumptious…"

"Hmm, pass then!" boomed the Ogre. (Who, to be honest, thought he'd heard this somewhere before.)

Eventually, all the Cowards used
the same trick to pass the Ogre. Who,
by now, had worked up a monstrous
appetite. "Where's my dinner?" he
howled.

"Down here!" cried Sir Lance-a-
Little, waving his tiny sword. "Try and
eat me if thee dare!"

"Huh?" grunted the Ogre.

He looked down at the brave – but
tiny – knight.

"You're no dinner!" he roared.
"You're not even a nibble!"

And with that, the disappointed Ogre stomped off downriver in a huff.

"It'll have to be Fisherman Pie for supper," he grumbled. "Or maybe Shepherd Pie…"

That great ugly brute
Found brave knights quite yummy.
But little Sir Lance
Would not fill his tummy!

Sir Lance-a-Little checked his Quest List again. "We must win a JOUSTING TOURNAMENT!" he cried.

The knights rode to the town of Little Riding, where the 'Joust-a-Minute' Jousting Tournament was taking place.

"Perfect," said Sir Lance-a-Little.

WELCOME
to ye
"JOUST-a-MINUTE"
JOUSTING
TOURNAMENT!
Sponsored by
Shield & Armour Insurance

Now, a knight can't joust without
a valiant steed to joust upon.

(A valiant steed is fancy knight talk
for a horse.)

So it was that Sir Lance-a-Little
entered the tournament on his, er…
Shetland Pony.

The other colourful knights in the
tournament looked at his small pony.

"Art thou feeling a little horse?" the Green Knight giggled.

"As knights go, thou art surely the shortest!" the Red Knight laughed.

"We'll see who laugheth the longest," replied Sir Lance-a-Little.

A fanfare sounded. The tournament began…

"Oh, dear…" said Sir Render, as the Cowards looked on.

But, guess what?

Sir Lance-a-Little was so small – none of the other knights could spike him.

And the other knights were so big – the little knight couldn't miss them.

Lo and behold...

SIR LANCE-A-LITTLE WON!

The Green Knight was hugely envious.

The Red Knight was greatly embarrassed.

And the Black and Blue Knights were bruised all over.

"The bigger they are, the harder they falleth!" smiled Sir Lance-a-Little.

> *The Knights thought our Lance*
> *Was a bit of a joke –*
> *Till he gave them the punch line*
> *With a little lance poke!*

"Just one more task!" exclaimed Sir Lance-a-Little, holding his Quest List up high.

"What is it?"

"Guess..."

② Rescue Damsel in Distress

① Banish evil wizard ☑

③ Conqu

"Give us a clue," said the Cowards.

"It rhymes with FLAGON," replied the little knight.

"Oh, dear..." said Sir Render.

④ Win Jousting Tournament

⑤ Slay a beast that rhymes with flagon →

They rode (reluctantly) until they came to a mountain.

In the side of the mountain…was a great, dark cave.

And in the great, dark cave lived… (well, you can guess).

"I'm going in!" cried Sir Lance-a-Little.

"We're going home!" whimpered the Cowards of Camelot.

"BE STILL, BRAVE KNIGHTS!" ordered the little knight.

So the Cowards of Camelot stood
at the great, dark cave entrance and
waited…

"COME OUT, THOU FIRE-BREATHING DRAGON!" yelled Sir Lance-a-Little. "THESE KNIGHTS BE NOT AFRAID!" (Which, as we know, wasn't strictly true.)

Out stomped the fierce dragon.

Amazingly, the Cowards of Camelot didn't run away (because they were frozen with fear).

"I'LL SKEWER YOU KNIGHTS AND BARBECUE MYSELF A CAMELOT KEBAB!" roared the dragon.

The knights quivered like jellies.

"OR MAYBE I'LL ROAST YOU SIRS LIKE SIR-LOIN STEAKS!"

The knights' knees knocked together.

But – while the dragon was unleashing its (fiery) temper – Sir Lance-a-Little sneaked around the back of the cave. And as the dragon was about to breathe a scorching blast of fire…the tiny knight pulled out his little lance and jabbed the dragon – in the bum!

"WHAT?!!!!?"

The dragon was so surprised… instead of breathing fire out – it sucked fire in!

"MY QUEST FOR BRAVERY IS OVER!" cried Sir Lance-a-Little, making one final tick before rolling up his list. "Now, I must hurry back to my master."

"Your master?" asked the Cowards. "Who is your master?"

"THE BLACK PRINCIPAL!" replied Sir Lance-a-Little.

The Cowards went all a-quiver.
For the Black Principal had a dark
reputation…for handing out terrible
punishments. But if they wanted
their rewards, the Cowards had to
accompany Sir Lance-a-Little back
to a tall, dark castle.

There, Sir Lance-a-Little knocked on
a tall, dark door – which was answered
by a tall, dark stranger.

It was THE BLACK PRINCIPAL!

But the Cowards of Camelot noticed something…

"Sir Lance-a-Little is scared, too!" they whispered.

And he was. His little teeth were a-chattering.

The Black Principal looked down at the tiny knight. "Have you completed your quest, Sir Lance-a-Little?"

There was a pause. (A short one.)

"Yes, Sir," replied Sir Lance-a-Little. "I've finished my bravery homework."

He handed over his Quest List.

"Then you shan't be terribly punished!" said the Black Principal.

"HOMEWORK!" cried the Cowards of Camelot. "You mean he's still at school?"

"Yes," said The Black Principal. "KNIGHT SCHOOL!"

To reward Sir Lance-a-Little for completing his bravery project, the Black Principal gave him a gold star.

And to thank the Cowards of Camelot for helping, the Black Principal gave them (can you guess?) – cake!

And what became of Sir Lance-a-Little?
Well, that's another story...

JOIN THE
POCKET HEROES

FOR SOME REALLY BIG ADVENTURES!

Join LOW-stature pirate Short John Silver in a HIGH-seas quest!

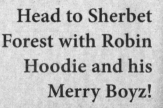

Head to Sherbet Forest with Robin Hoodie and his Merry Boyz!

Fight the power in ancient Rome with Junior Caesar!

Clean up fairy-tale land with Florence Nightingirl and her National Elf Service!

Bring football home with pint-sized-prince, Henry 1/8th!

COLLECT THEM ALL!

Fairy Tale Twists

Written by Katie Dale
Illustrated by Matt Buckingham

All priced at £8.99

Orchard Books are available from all good bookshops,
or can be ordered from our website, www.orchardbooks.co.uk,
or telephone 01235 827702, or fax 01235 827703.

DAVE WOODS
CHRIS INNS

SHORT JOHN SILVER	978 1 40831 359 6
SIR LANCE-A-LITTLE	978 1 40831 360 2
ROBIN HOODIE	978 1 40831 364 0
JUNIOR CAESAR	978 1 40831 362 6
FLORENCE NIGHTINGIRL	978 1 40831 363 3
HENRY THE 1/8TH	978 1 40831 361 9

All softbacks priced at £4.99

Orchard Books are available from all good bookshops,
or can be ordered from our website: www.orchardbooks.co.uk,
or telephone 01235 827702, or fax 01235 827703.